This book belongs to:

....

To my beloved Joel
and
my three children Cole, Koral, and Carson
"143Myfamily"

Publisher's Cataloging-in-Publication data

Names: Pattison, Kimberly Pellerin, author. | Dural, Zeynep, illustrator.
Title: I'm not scared , no way : I'm getting my haircut today / written by Kimberly Pattison;
Illustrated by Zeynep Dural.
Description: Kimberly Pattison, 2022. |
Summary: Carson is scared of getting his hair cut but he pushes through his fear and likes his new look.
Identifiers: LCCN: 2022913748 | ISBN: 979-8-9864829-1-0 (hardcover) | 979-8-9864829-0-3 (paperback)
Subjects: LCSH Haircutting--Juvenile fiction. | Fear--Juvenile fiction. | Self-reliance--Juvenile fiction. |
BISAC JUVENILE FICTION / Social Themes / Emotions & Feelings | JUVENILE FICTION /
Social Themes / New Experience
Classification: LCC PZ7.1 .P3772 Im 2022 | DDC [E]--dc23

Illustrations by Zeynep Dural
Cover Design by Praise Saflor
Format and Layout by Glaiza Beverly Ganaba

I'M NOT SCARED NO WAY!

Written by
Kimberly Pattison

Illustrated by
Zeynep Dural

I'm not scared, no **WAY!**
I'm getting my hair cut today!

I'm not scared **NUH-UH!**
I bet when I'm done we can play.

My mom says my hair looks shaggy,
so she made an appointment with Miss Maggy.

I'm beginning to feel **SCARED**, I say.
I don't want to get my hair cut today.
Yep, I'm scared, uh huh.
I don't even want to play.

We get in the car,
but we don't drive far.

Mom says, "Carson, there's no need to fear.
LOOK, we're already here."

Into the salon we go,
and I'm walking really **SLOW**.

I climb on Miss Maggy's chair
and she softly combs my hair.
A little **SNIP** here and a little **SNIP** there.
Then she slowly lowers the chair.

Miss Maggy says, "We're all done. Now, wasn't that **FUN**?

Yep, you're all through,
And boy look at **YOU**?"

HEY, Mom, look at me!
I can't wait for my dad to see.
Best of all, I still look like ME!

I'm not scared, nuh uh!
Now me and Cooper can **PLAY!**

CERTIFICATE
FIRST HAIRCUT

This is to certify that

....

has bravely met all the
requirements of receiving their
FIRST HAIRCUT
on the .... of ...... in the year of ....

by: ....

PHOTO

HERE

AUTHOR

Kimberly Pellerin Pattison has been a hairdresser for 35 years. She has witnessed firsthand the fear young children can express at the thought of getting their first haircut.

Having been a mother to three and now a (Sweetie) to her grandchildren she is reminded of the importance of talking to children about their potentially scary life events.

Kimberly was drawn to writing this book hoping to show children that it's okay to feel fear but it's even better to conquer those fears.

She also hopes this book reminds parents to teach their children "THERE'S NOTHING THEY CAN'T DO."

This book will also be a great keepsake with placement in the back for a lock of your child's hair and a certificate of achievement.

Zeynep Dural was born in Istanbul, Turkey in 1989. She has bachelor's degree in "Cartoon and Animations".

In addition, she has studied children's book illustration and received an MA Children's Book Certificate from Anglia Ruskin University, UK.

While conducting her studies, she worked as a freelance illustrator and designer for different animation studios and children's book publishers .

She has illustrated more than 20 books and keeps writing and illustrating her very own picturebooks as well. She is still working as freelance Illustrator and living in Coventry, UK with her husband and two cats.

ILLUSTRATOR

THANK YOU!

Thank you for reading our book!
If you loved it, please consider leaving a review.

Some Freebies For You!

Visit us at kimberlypattison.com to get additional resources and freebies. We will also keep you up to date with new offerings and updates.

88745616R00017